BABY-SITTERS LITTLE SISTER®

Karen's New Year

BABY SITTERS
LITTLE SISTER

Karen's New Year

ANN M. MARTIN

ILLUSTRATIONS BY HEATHER BURNS

SCHOLASTIC INC.

For everyone who needs
a new beginning

Copyright © 1991 by Ann M. Martin

This book was originally published in paperback in 1991.

All rights reserved. Published by Scholastic Inc., *Publishers since 1920*. SCHOLASTIC, BABY-SITTERS LITTLE SISTER, and associated logos are trademarks and/or registered trademarks of Scholastic Inc.

The publisher does not have any control over and does not assume any responsibility for author or third-party websites or their content.

ISBN 978-1-338-87564-5

10 9 8 7 6 5 4 3 2 1   24 25 26 27 28

Printed in the U.S.A. 40
This edition first printing 2024

Book design by Maeve Norton

CHAPTER 1

It was December 26th. It was the day after Christmas. Usually when I wake up on the day after Christmas I feel a little sad. That is because my favorite holiday is over. But then I remember something. I remember the toys and presents I got the day before. That makes me feel better. Sometimes I even feel excited.

My name is Karen Brewer, and I finally turned seven years old. I have blonde hair and some freckles. I wear glasses — all the time. I have a little brother, too. His name is Andrew. He is almost five. Sometimes he is a pain in the neck, but mostly I like him.

My mommy and daddy are divorced.

Here are some of the things I got for

Christmas: lots of books, a doll called Baby Grow-a-Tooth, leg warmers that my Nannie knitted for me, a special art kit, some clothes, and a game called *Sorry!*

Andrew got a hat that Nannie knitted him, these exploding Dyno-cars, an art kit like mine, and some other stuff.

When I thought about my presents, I leaped out of bed. I put on all new clothes: a very short skirt, a big sweater that says BE COOL on it, and a pair of knee socks with snowflakes all over them. (I had not gotten new shoes, so I did not put any shoes on.)

In the morning, Andrew and I sat around the living room. We played with our toys and looked at our books. At eleven o'clock, my friend Nancy Dawes came over. She lives next door. She brought *her* Baby Grow-a-Tooth with her. She had gotten Baby Grow-a-Tooth for Hanukkah.

"Cool," I said. "Our dolls can grow teeth together."

Crash, smash! That was Andrew. He had run a car into the wall and it had exploded. (The car, I mean. Not the wall.) Andrew put the car back together and then crashed it and exploded it again.

Ring, ring! The telephone. "I'll get it!" I cried.

I ran into the kitchen and answered the phone.

"Hi, sweetie. It's Daddy," said the voice at the other end of the line.

"Hi, Daddy! Andrew and Nancy and I are playing with our new toys."

"That sounds like fun," said Daddy. "Listen, is your mom there? I was thinking of having a party on New Year's Eve. It would be just the family — Nannie and Kristy and your stepbrothers and everyone. Do you think you and Andrew could come?"

I paused. I was not sure. Sometimes Mommy and Daddy fight over who Andrew and I spend holidays with. "Let me get Mommy," I said.

So I did. And I got prepared for an argument. But there was no argument. You know what Mommy said? She said, "That would be fine. Seth" (he's my stepfather) "and I have been wanting to go skiing. Do you think you could take Karen and Andrew for several days? That way, they could go to the party, and Seth and I could go skiing."

Of course Daddy said yes.

"Hurray!" I shouted.

"Indoor voice, Karen," Mommy reminded me. (She was still talking on the phone.)

"Sorry," I said. Then I ran into the living

room. "Guess what! Guess what!" I said, but not too loudly. "Daddy is having a New Year's Eve party at the big house, and we get to go, Andrew."

"Goody!" he said. He exploded a car.

Oh, boy. Now I had another holiday to look forward to.

CHAPTER 2

By now you are probably wondering a lot of things. I bet you are wondering what the big house is. I bet you are wondering why Mommy and Daddy have fights about the holidays. And I bet you are wondering who Nannie is.

Well, as I said before, Mommy and Daddy are divorced. They used to be married to each other. (That was when they had Andrew and me.) But now they are not married anymore. They both love Andrew and me very much, but they decided that they did not love each other.

So they got divorced.

But that was not the end of things. Then they

each got married again. Mommy married Seth, and Daddy married Elizabeth. Elizabeth is my stepmother.

When the divorce happened, Mommy moved Andrew and me out of Daddy's big house and into a little house. Then she and Seth got married, and Seth moved in. He brought his dog, Midgie, and his cat, Rocky, with him. (Oh, we have another pet — my rat, Emily Junior.) Things around the little house are pretty quiet.

The big house, where Daddy grew up, is *not* quiet! That is one reason I like it so much. First of all, Elizabeth has *four* children. They are Sam and Charlie, who are in high school; David Michael, who is seven like me; and Kristy. Kristy is thirteen and I love her very much. She is a baby-sitter. She even has her own sitting business. She is the president. Kristy is my favorite baby-sitter in the whole world. Guess what. At the big house, I also have a little sister. Her name is Emily Michelle. (I named my rat after her.) She was born in Vietnam. Emily is two and a half. She does not talk much. *Another* person at the big house is Nannie. I think of her as my grandmother, even though she is Elizabeth's mother. That makes her my step-grandmother. Nannie moved in to take care of Emily while Daddy and Elizabeth are at work. *Plus*, there are a cat and a dog at the big house. Boo-Boo is Daddy's old cat. He spits and scratches. Shannon is David Michael's puppy.

You know what? I call my brother Andrew Two-Two. I call myself Karen Two-Two. That is because we have two of so many things. (I got the name from a book that my teacher read us. It is called *Jacob Two-Two Meets the Hooded Fang*.) Andrew and I have two houses. We live with Mommy and Seth most of the time. We live at Daddy's big house every other weekend. We have two mothers, two fathers, two dogs, and two cats. I even have two best friends. Nancy Dawes lives next door to Mommy. Hannie

Papadakis lives across the street and one house down from Daddy. Hannie and Nancy and I call ourselves the Three Musketeers.

Andrew and I have two of lots of other things. We have toys and books and games and clothes at each house. I have a bicycle at each house, and Andrew has a tricycle at each house. Plus I have two stuffed cats that are just the same, except for their names. Moosie stays at the big house, and Goosie stays at the little house. Being two-twos is mostly okay. We do not have to remember to pack much when we go back and forth between houses.

But some things about being two-twos are not okay. I only had one special blanket, Tickly. I kept leaving Tickly behind at one house or the other. Finally I had to rip Tickly in half so I could have a piece at each house. (I hope that did not hurt Tickly.) Then there is the problem with holidays. Mommy and Daddy both want to celebrate all the holidays with us. Usually we end up having two holidays. But sometimes Mommy and Daddy fight.

That was why I was so happy when Mommy let Andrew and me go to the big house for New Year's Eve. No fighting!

CHAPTER 3

After Andrew had exploded his car and put it back together again, he looked at me. "What's New Year's Eve?" he asked.

What's New Year's Eve? I could not believe that Andrew did not know that, since he is almost five.

"It's the last night of the old year, and twelve o'clock is the beginning of a new year. It is very, very important," I said.

"Does it always happen right after Christmas?" Andrew wondered.

I glanced at Nancy. She shrugged. She could not believe that Andrew did not know about New Year's Eve, either.

"Yup," I said to Andrew. "It always happens a week after Christmas."

"Why?"

"Because Christmas is near the end of December. And December is the last month of the year. Then comes January. That's the first month of the next year. Here. I'll get a calendar and show you."

"Well, I think I'll be going now," said Nancy. She grabbed Baby Grow-a-Tooth. Then she put on her coat and hat and mittens and boots. I guess she did not want to hear a calendar lesson.

I ran upstairs to my room and took my calendar off of the wall. I brought it down to Andrew.

"This," I said to Andrew, "is a calendar. It keeps track of the days of the year. See these boxes?"

"Yes," said Andrew, frowning.

"Each one stands for a day."

"How come you make lines across the boxes?"

"I do that at the end of each day. Then I

can tell which day we're up to. Anyway, don't worry about that. Now see how the boxes are all arranged on a page?"

"Yup."

"Well, each page is a month."

"What's a month?"

Oh, brother, I thought. Then I said, "When's your birthday, Andrew?"

He told me.

"Good," I said. "This is the month. And this is the day of the month. It's your birthday." I turned the calendar to Andrew's birthday and showed him where it was. "And your birthday is always the same. Just like Christmas is always the same. December twenty-fifth. See? Here it is on the calendar."

"Okay," said Andrew. "And New Year's Eve?"

"Last day of the year," I replied.

"Last day! We've never, ever had a last day. Every day is followed by another one. I don't want New Year's Eve if it will be the last day."

I sighed.

"*Is* it the last day?" Andrew asked.

"No. It really is not." I explained New Year's Eve to Andrew all over again. I was very, very patient with him.

Then I said, "Guess how we will celebrate New Year's Eve at Daddy's."

"With calendars?" Andrew suggested.

"No! With a big party. We will probably get to stay up until midnight. That's *twelve o'clock*. And we will blow horns and toss confetti into the air. Maybe we will throw streamers around, too."

"Really? Oh, boy!" cried Andrew. "A party. A party at the big house."

"And what are we celebrating?" I asked him.

"The last day?"

I sighed again. "No," I said. "But we will have a gigundo fun party."

CHAPTER 4

December 30th was the day before the very last day of the year. And Mommy and Seth were leaving. They were going on their ski trip. They were going to the state of New Hampshire. That is a little bit far away.

"You two," said Mommy to Andrew and me, "will stay with Daddy until January third. That's four days. That's also the day school begins again. Karen, that morning, Daddy will take you to school. Andrew, you will stay at the big house with Nannie and Emily. In the afternoon, Seth will pick up Andrew at Daddy's and I will pick up Karen at school. Do you understand the plans?"

"Yup!" I said. I was so happy. A New Year's Eve party, and four days with my big-house family!

"Andrew, do you understand?" asked Mommy.

Andrew just nodded. The corners of his mouth turned down. He was trying not to cry. Sometimes four days at the big house is too much for Andrew.

"Is everybody ready?" called Seth. Seth had been packing our station wagon. He had put his suitcase and Mommy's suitcase into it. He had put my backpack and Andrew's backpack into it. And he had put the skis on top of the car.

"We're ready!" I cried. "I can't wait!"

Seth drove us to the big house. Mommy got out of the car so she could say good-bye to Andrew and me.

"Have lots of fun," she said.

"We will!" I adjusted my backpack. "Bye, Mommy!" I kissed her.

Then Andrew kissed her.

"See you later, alligators," said Mommy.

"After awhile, crocodile," I replied as Mommy got into the car.

Andrew did not say anything. Tears were rolling down his cheeks.

I walked Andrew into the big house. Everybody came to greet us. But Andrew just stood in the hallway and cried. I put my arm around him.

"Don't worry," I said. "We're going to have fun. And Mommy will be back in four days. That's not very long."

"I know." Andrew sniffled. Then Daddy gave him a big hug.

"Who wants to come with me to buy party stuff?" called Charlie. Charlie can drive, and he has his own car. He is very proud of it, even though it is a wreck. It always looks like it is going to fall apart.

"I do!" cried David Michael and Kristy and I.

And Andrew stopped crying. "Party stuff?" he said.

"Yeah," replied Charlie. "You know, popcorn and hats and confetti and horns and streamers."

"Chocolate candy?" asked Andrew.

"Sure," said Charlie.

"Can I invite Hannie to come with us?" I asked. "I know she's not coming to the party. But she likes to go shopping."

Charlie said, "Sure," to that, too. (He usually says "Sure.")

So I called Hannie, and she ran right over.

Then we piled into Charlie's Junk Bucket. (That is what Sam calls the car.) We drove downtown. We went into a dollar store. Almost nothing in the store costs a dollar. But we found everything we wanted. Even chocolate for Andrew.

"This is so, so fun," I said to Kristy.

"I know," she replied, smiling. "The party will be great. Now all we have to do is think up New Year's resolutions."

Huh? I thought. What are they?

CHAPTER 5

I did not have time to ask Kristy about the resolutions. We were too busy in the store. We had baskets full of things, and we had to pay for them.

Then David Michael wanted gum from the gumball machine, and Andrew wanted some M&Ms from the candy machine, and Hannie and I both wanted rings with spiders on them from the toy machine. So that took awhile.

But when we were at home again, and Hannie had gone back to her house, I said to Kristy, "What is a New Year's resolution?"

Kristy and I were in the kitchen. We were putting away the things we had bought. I was wearing my new spider ring.

"A resolution," Kristy began, "is a deci-sion. But a New Year's resolution is more like a promise. A promise about something you will change."

"I don't understand," I said.

"A promise to change something in your life. To make your life better. You might resolve to break a bad habit. Or you might resolve to start exercising every day."

"Oh!" I said. "Cool! Do you make just one resolution?"

"Usually, I guess," replied Kristy. "But some people make lots of resolutions."

"Okay. I better go tell everyone else. We should all decide on resolutions before the party tomorrow night."

I told all the people in the big house (even Emily) about resolutions. And everyone (except Emily) said that they would announce their resolutions at the party. (Emily did not understand resolutions.)

Oh, well. *I* was excited. This is great! I thoug

I like to make lists. I like to make promises and keep them.

I decided Hannie better make a resolution, too. So I went over to her house.

I rang her bell.

Hannie's older brother answered the door. "Hi, Musketeer," said Linny. (He knows about the Three Musketeers.)

"Hi. Is —"

"She's up in her room," Linny told me, before I could even finish my question.

"Okay. Thanks." I ran upstairs to Hannie's room. I found her sitting on the floor, playing with Sari, her little sister.

"Hi!" said Hannie when she saw me. "I'm teaching Sari how to sing 'Old MacDonald Had a Farm.'"

"*E-I-E-I-O,*" said Sari proudly.

"That's great. But listen, Hannie, I just found out something important. We have to make New Year's resolutions."

I explained about resolutions to Hannie.

Then I said, "What will your resolution be? This is serious."

Hannie thought and thought. Finally she said, "I am going to stop biting my nails."

"Oh, that's a good one!" I exclaimed. "I can't decide on a resolution. I can think of so many. But Kristy said most people only make one resolution."

"That's *most* people," said Hannie. "How come you can't make a whole list? Like a list of birthday presents."

"Maybe I could," I said slowly. "I better go home. I have to solve this problem. Good luck with your nails, Hannie."

"Thanks," she said. "Bye, Karen."

"Bye!"

"*E-I-E-I-O!*" sang Sari.

CHAPTER 6

When I got back to the big house, I could not make a decision. Should I make one resolution or a list of resolutions?

"Why don't you sleep on it?" suggested Kristy. "Think about it tonight, decide tomorrow."

So I did that. And on the next day I decided that I would make a list of resolutions. Since it was New Year's Day, our party would be that night.

I better get right to work, I thought.

I sat down at the table in my bedroom. Pencils and a pad of paper were on the table. I began to write. This is the list I made:

1. I will not eat sweets.
2. I will be helpful with Emily.

3. I will not stay up past my bedtime, even to read.
4. I will tell Ricky Torres that he has to ask me to marry him.
5. I will not make any spelling mistakes.
6. I will not pester Boo Boo.
7. I will, share my toys with Andrew.
8. I will do something nice for someone every day.
9. I will be nicer to Morbidda Destiny.

(Morbidda Destiny is an old lady who lives next door to Daddy. I am pretty sure she is a witch.)

I tried and tried to think of a tenth resolution, but I could not. I really wanted to. Ten resolutions would be a nice round number.

Oh, well. I looked at my list. Maybe I could narrow it down. Maybe I should choose ju

one resolution. Everyone else would probably make only one. I read my list again. No. I could not leave out anything. All the resolutions were important.

I knew I would have to work hard to keep my resolutions. For instance, I would have to check *all* of my spelling very, very carefully. And I would have to think of something nice to do someone each day. That might be difficult.

And probably I would not always want to share with Andrew. But I would do it anyway.

I knew I had made the best promises of all.

I could not wait to read my list at the party that night.

Everyone would be very impressed.

I was going to start off the new year in a big way.

CHAPTER 7

We had a gigundo fun dinner that night.

"Last dinner of the old year!" said Elizabeth.

"But there will be another dinner tomorrow ... won't there?" asked Andrew. Tears filled his eyes again.

"Oh, of course, honey," said Elizabeth. She put her arm around Andrew. "But it will be the *first* dinner of the *new* year."

At dinner, we ate ham and baked potatoes and peas with *sauce* on them. For dessert, Elizabeth made a big fruit salad. We ate and talked about our party. We remembered funny things that had happened during the year. We said what we wanted to happen during the new year. Mostly we wanted peace and *no guns*.

When dinner was over, I said, "Let's go into the living room now. Let's tell our resolutions!"

So we did. We sat on couches or chairs or the floor. All of us. Even Emily. But Emily played with toys and did not pay attention to what was going on.

"Who should go first?" I asked.

"Oldest to youngest," replied Nannie. "I will go first. Here is my resolution. I resolve to work very hard to make my hip better." (Nannie broke her hip last month.) "I bet I will be walking on my own even before the doctors say I will."

Daddy went next. "I resolve to lose ten pounds by April." He patted his tummy. "I'm getting —"

"A gut?" suggested Sam, and everyone laughed.

"I," began Elizabeth, "resolve to finish things I start."

"I resolve not to talk on the phone while I'm doing my homework," said Charlie.

"I resolve not to burp loudly at the table anymore," said Sam.

"Ew, gross!" I cried. "Sam, that's not a resolution."

"Do you want me to keep burping?" he asked.

"No," I replied.

"Okay, so that's my resolution."

Then Kristy resolved not to talk about softball while she was on the phone with Bart. Bart is Kristy's boyfriend, I guess. They both coach softball teams. But it seems like all they ever *do* is talk about softball.

"I resolve," said David Michael, "to practice hitting and pitching every day."

"Good for you," said Kristy. (David Michael is on her team.) "Karen, what's your resolution?" she asked.

"I want to go last," I told her.

So Andrew resolved to floss his teeth every night, which made Sam laugh, which made ndrew cry.

But I saved the day. I read my list of resolutions.

"You're going to do *all* those things?" said Kristy. She raised her eyebrows.

"Yup," I replied. "*And* I am going to make resolutions *for* Shannon and Boo-Boo and Emily," I went on.

"Not Emily," Daddy interrupted. "She's too little. I don't want you to expect her to do something she doesn't understand. If you want to make resolutions for Shannon and Boo-Boo, go ahead. But don't expect them to keep promises."

"Okay," I replied. "I resolve that Shannon will not have any more accidents in the house. And I resolve that Boo-Boo will not scratch anymore."

I was done. We cheered for ourselves. Everyone was feeling proud.

CHAPTER 8

Par-*ty!*" yelled Sam. "Let's get this New Year's Eve party going!"

"Let's get the food!" said David Michael.

Our resolutions were over. The serious part of the evening was over. So we brought out some of our party food.

"Now what?" asked Andrew.

"Let's play games," said David Michael.

"Games that Nannie can play, too," added Charlie.

We played Twenty Questions and Memory. Then I suggested a spelling bee, but nobody wanted to do that. So we played Categories. Then Sam turned on the TV to see the New Year's Eve parties in New York City. At one, a big band was playing. We began to dance around the living room. Except for Nannie, who couldn't, and Emily, who had fallen asleep.

"How could she fall asleep when we're being so noisy?" I asked.

"She's only two," said Nannie gently.

Elizabeth carried Emily Michelle upstairs to put her to bed.

"What time is it?" I asked.

"Ten-thirty," Kristy replied.

"Only ten-thirty?!" The night seemed *very* long.

At eleven, Elizabeth made popcorn. At eleven-thirty, Sam found a different station on the TV.

"There's the ball," he exclaimed. He was looking at a lighted ball way up high on a tower or something. "At eleven fifty-nine," he said, "that will start to fall. When it reaches the bottom, it will be the new year."

"Why?" asked Andrew. He looked confused (Also sleepy.)

Sam tried to explain. But he did not get far. Daddy and Elizabeth were handing out hats. They put bags of confetti and piles of streamers on the coffee table. "It's almost time!" said Daddy.

Soon the TV announcer said, "It's eleven fifty-nine, folks!"

When ten seconds were left, we counted backwards to zero. ". . . three, two, one, zero! . . . Happy New Year!"

"Yay! Hurray!" Everyone shouted and screamed and hugged. We threw confetti and streamers everywhere. We blew our horns.

The room was gigundo noisy.

"Come on," said Daddy. "Let's open the front door."

We did. And all up and down the street we could hear people shouting, "Happy New Year!" and blowing horns. It was exciting.

But soon Elizabeth said, "Bedtime."

Before I knew it, I was in bed. I was very tired, but I could not sleep. I had brought some Hershey's Kisses up to my room. Maybe candy would help me sleep. I was reaching for one when I remembered my first resolution: *I will not eat sweets*.

I drew my hand back quickly. I would have to remember to put the candies away the next day.

Then a horrible thought occurred to me. I was up *way* past my bedtime. Had I already broken my third resolution? I decided I had not

Daddy and Elizabeth had given all of us permission to stay up until after midnight.

But I realized just how hard it would be to keep my resolutions. It would be even harder than I had thought.

Boo.

CHAPTER 9

Guess how late I slept the next morning. Eleven o'clock! I was gigundo glad that I had not made a resolution about sleeping late. I would have broken it for sure.

I got dressed quickly. I made my bed. Then I thought — what could be the nice thing that I do for someone today? The answer was easy. I had already done it. I had made my bed. (I do not always remember to. Then Daddy or Elizabeth gets cross and has to remind me.)

Feeling very proud of myself, I went downstairs. I was starving! Should I eat breakfast or lunch? I wondered. The first meal of the day is usually breakfast. But it was almost lunchtime.

When I got to the kitchen, Sam, K

Daddy, Andrew, and David Michael were there. They were sitting at the table.

"Morning, sweetie," said Daddy.

"Morning," I replied. "What meal is this?"

"It's brunch," said Kristy, grinning. "We're eating whenever we wake up."

"What's brunch?" I asked.

"Breakfast *and* lunch at the same time," David Michael told me. "Get it? Breakfast and lunch? Brunch?"

"Yeah!" I said. "Neat."

Daddy served me eggs and fruit and a muffin. "What do you want to drink?" he asked. "You can have anything you want."

Before I could answer, we all heard a loud, "B-U-R-P!"

"Excuse me," said Sam.

"Sam!" I cried. "You already broke your resolution! You didn't keep it for a day. You didn't keep it at *all*. This is your first meal of the new ar. And you burped."

orry," said Sam. (He did not sound very

sorry.) "I really needed to burp. I drank my soda too fast. Besides, when I made my resolution, I meant I would not burp just to gross people out."

"Well, you didn't say so."

"Well, that's what I *meant*."

"Okay, okay," said Daddy. "Enough arguing."

I didn't say anything else to Sam during brunch — even though he did not burp again. But I had a plan.

As soon as I finished eating, I went to my room and found a notebook. I turned to the first page and wrote *SAM* at the top. Underneath that I wrote: *Jan. 1 — Sam burped loudly at brunch.*

While I was doing that, I reached over to my dresser. I felt around until I found a piece of gum. I unwrapped it and put it into my mouth. I chewed slowly while I wrote about Sam.

Then suddenly — uh-oh! I was chewing *gum!*

Gum is a sweet, isn't it?

I grabbed the gum wrapper and read it. *Sugarless gum*, it said.

WHEW. I decided I was safe. If the gum was sugarless, then it was not a sweet. And I was not in trouble.

But Sam was.

And I decided I better keep an eye on everyone else. Maybe they would not be any better at keeping resolutions than Sam was. I was glad my notebook was thick. I might need a lot of pages.

I hid the gum in my nightgown drawer. *I* knew I was keeping my first resolution, but if someone else saw the gum, they might not think so.

CHAPTER 10

"*There was a farmer had a dog and Bingo was his name-o. B-I-N-G-O, B-I-N-G-O, B-I-N-G-O, and Bingo was his name-o.*"

It was the next day. I was so, so happy that I was still at the big house. I was in our playroom. I was pretending I was a farmer. I had found a straw hat, and I was wearing overalls and a plaid shirt. I was trying to make Shannon be my dog, but she did not want to play.

Ring, ring! went the telephone.

"I'll get it!" I cried.

But Kristy was saying, "I'll get it," too — and she did.

She stood in the hall outside the playroom

I could not help overhearing her end of the conversation.

"Hi, Bart!" she said happily. There was a pause. Then Kristy said, "No, I think it's too cold for a game. Anyway, it's supposed to snow on Monday. . . Yeah. . . Yeah. What? The kids' hats? . . . Oh, their *bats*. I guess we could find some aluminum bats. That shouldn't be a problem . . . No, it's a good idea. I'm glad you called. Okay, I'll talk to you soon. Bye!"

Well.

I could not believe it. Now *Kristy* had broken her resolution. And resolutions had been her idea in the first place.

I ran into the hall.

"Kristy!" I said.

"Yes, Farmer Jones?"

"I'm not Farmer Jones. And you broke your resolution."

"What?" said Kristy.

"You *broke* your resolution. You talked about ball on the phone with Bart."

"Well, I couldn't help it," replied Kristy. She sounded huffy. "Bart *called* to talk about softball stuff. When I made my resolution, I just meant that we wouldn't talk about softball when we're having a friendly, casual conversation. Because we should learn to talk about other things. But Bart had some questions. What was I supposed to do? Tell him he has to come over because I can't answer his questions on the phone?"

"I guess not," I said slowly. "Sorry, Kristy."

"That's okay," she replied. But she looked a little cross.

Kristy went back to her room. I took off my hat. Then I went to my room, too. I found the notebook I had started. I turned past Sam's page. On the next page, I wrote KRISTY. Underneath that I wrote: *Jan. 2 — Kristy talked about softball on the phone with Bart.*

Boy. People sure didn't take their resolutions seriously. I decided to go over to Hannie's house. I would complain to her. Hannie always liste~ when someone complains. That is very har~

At the Papadakises' house, Linny let me in and told me that Hannie was upstairs in her room reading. I decided to tiptoe upstairs and surprise her.

When I did, guess what I found. Hannie was lying on her bed, reading a book.

She was biting her nails.

"Hannie!" I cried.

Hannie jumped a mile. "Karen! I didn't hear you come in."

"Hannie, you broke your New Year's resolution. You're biting your nails."

"Oops," said Hannie. But she did not seem upset.

When I went home later, I started a page for Hannie in my notebook. I wrote: *Jan. 2 — Hannie was biting her nails.*

CHAPTER 11

Sometime in the afternoon that day, I remembered that I was supposed to do something nice for someone. So I made Andrew's bed for him. I did not even tell him that I had done it.

Then that night, I remembered that I had resolved to be helpful with Emily. So I said to Daddy and Elizabeth, "Tonight I will put Emily Michelle to bed for you."

"How nice," said Daddy.

"Thank you," said Elizabeth.

Then Daddy added, "Remember to put a diaper on her."

"Okay," I replied. (We are toilet-training Emily. She wears panties during the da Usually she does not have accidents. At ni she still wears a diaper, though. And I know how to put one on her.)

I took Emily by the hand. I led her around to all the people in the big house. "Night-night," said Emily to each one.

Then I walked Emily upstairs to her room. Emily used to have a crib. Now she has a big-girl bed.

"Let's read a story first," I said to Emily.

I sat her on the bed and found her copy of *Peter Rabbit*. Then I sat next to her. I opened the book and began to read.

We had just reached the part where Peter gets caught in the gooseberry net, when Emily said, "Uh-oh."

I did not like the sound of her "uh-oh."

"What?" I asked her.

"Wet," said Emily.

"*Oh*," I groaned. I lifted her up. Emily had wet her pants. She had wet right through her blue ʲans, and the blanket and sheets on the bed.

"*Emily*," I said. I could not help sounding a little cross. Now I would have to clean up Emily *and* change her bed.

Emily began to cry.

"I'm sorry," I told her. "It's all right. It was an accident."

I took off Emily's wet clothes and put a diaper on her. Then I slipped her nightgown over her head. "Okay. *You're* ready." I turned a looked at the bed. I still had to change it. That was a much bigger job than changing Emily.

"Kristy!" I called.

"Yeah?" (Kristy was down the hall, reading to Andrew and David Michael.)

"Emily had an accident. I need you to help me change her bed."

"I'm busy," Kristy replied. "Besides, I thought one of your resolutions was to be more helpful with Emily."

"Never mind!" I shouted.

I changed the bed myself. It took a long time. Emily fell asleep on the floor while I was working. Then, when I finally put her to bed, I had to take the wet blankets and sheets down to the laundry room. When I was finished, I was very tired.

I went to my room. I looked around for my list of New Year's resolutions. I changed the second one to read, *I will be more helpful with Emily. except when she wets her pants.*

Then I called Daddy. When he came to my

room, I told him what had happened. I did not tell him I had changed my resolution. But I said, "It isn't fair that Emily didn't make a resolution. She should resolve not to wet her pants anymore."

"Sorry, sweetie," said Daddy. "Emily is too little for resolutions."

That was the end of that.

CHAPTER 12

I could not believe it. Christmas was over. New Year's Eve was over. And now our winter vacation was over.

It was time to go back to school.

Luckily, I like school. I did not mind going back. I like my teacher *very* much. Her name is Ms. Colman. And Hannie and Nancy and I are all in Ms. Colman's second-grade class.

Ms. Colman almost never yells. She is very patient with me. I am the youngest kid in my class and sometimes I forget things. I forget when to use my indoor voice and when to raise my hand. Ms. Colman reminds me nicely.

I like most of the other kids in my class, too. I have a friend named Natalie and a friend named Sara. But I especially like this boy named Ricky Torres. I used to call him Yicky Ricky. That was because he teased me when I got glasses. Now we both wear glasses, and Ricky has stopped teasing me.

I plan to marry him.

When I got to school on that first day after vacation, I marched right up to Ricky's desk. (He sits next to me in the front row.) I had to keep my fourth New Year's resolution.

"Ricky," I said. "Will you ask me to marry you?"

Ricky was sitting at his desk. He was coloring a picture of a spaceship. "Sure," he replied. He did not even look at me.

"You will?"

"Yup."

Goody! I could not wait.

Then I ran to the back of the room whe

Hannie and Nancy were talking and talking off their coats.

"Hi, you guys!" I said. The Three Musketeers were together again.

"Hi!" they replied.

We talked for a few minutes about our vacations. Then I said to Nancy, "Did you make a New Year's resolution?"

"Yes," replied Nancy, "even though this is the Jewish New Year. We celebrate that in the fall. But I resolved to stop passing notes to Hannie at school."

"Oh, that's good," I said. "I like that resolution."

Hannie sat down at her desk. She pawed through the junk in it with one hand. She bit the nails on her other hand.

"Hannie! You're biting your nails again!" I cried.

"Oh," said Hannie. She looked guilty.

I went right back to my desk. I pulled the notebook out of it. (I'd been carrying the notebook around with me.) On Hannie's page I wrote: *Jan. 3 — Hannie was biting her nails again.*

At recess, I realized something. Ricky had not asked me to marry him yet. I had to go find him. He was playing catch with Hank Reubens.

"Hey, Ricky!" I yelled. "Come here!"

Ricky tossed the ball to Hank. Then he ran to me. "Yeah?" he said.

"You haven't asked me to marry you yet."

"I know."

"Well?"

"Well, I didn't say *when* I would ask you," Ricky replied.

I felt grumpy. No one was keeping their promises.

It was not fair.

CHAPTER 13

After recess, we went back to our classroom. We never know what to expect then. Sometimes Ms. Colman has work for us. Sometimes she has a fun project for us. Sometimes she reads to us.

That day, she read.

"Class," began Ms. Colman, "since it's the beginning of a new year, I thought we should start a new book. This is the book that I picked out."

Ms. Colman held up a copy of *Doctor Dolittle*.

"I know that book!" I cried without raising my hand.

"Indoor voice, Karen," said Ms. Colman. "And please remember to raise your hand."

"Sorry," I said. "Anyway, it's a story about a man who can talk to animals."

"That's right," said Ms. Colman. And she began to read.

The story was *so* good that I turned around in my seat. I wanted to see how Hannie and Nancy liked it. Guess what. Their hands were joined. They were passing a note!

I swung around and pulled my notebook out of my desk. On Nancy's page I wrote: *Jan. 3 — Nancy passed a note to Hannie in school.*

I . . . WAS . . . MAD.

But when I asked them about it after school, Hannie said, "*I* passed the note, Karen. Nancy kept her resolution."

I did not believe her.

That night, Andrew and I were back at the little house. I was so, so happy to see Mommy and Seth again. So was Andrew. We had a very nice dinner together. Then I did my homework.

I was in the middle of a hard arithmetic problem when I heard Mommy say, "Time to get ready for bed, Andrew."

I jumped up. I knew what he would do first — brush his teeth.

I stood outside the door to the bathroom and listened. When I heard Andrew spit out his toothpaste, I peeked in the bathroom.

Andrew did not floss his teeth!

Okay, I thought. Andrew isn't keeping his resolution, either. I tiptoed back to my bedroom. I made a page for Andrew and wrote: *Jan. 3 — Andrew did not floss his teeth after dinner.*

While I was writing, I chewed a piece of Bazooka bubble gum. Suddenly something occurred to me. Was *this* gum sugarless? No!

Now what had I done?

I had broken my first resolution for *real*. Oh, well. I would just change it. Kristy had not said you couldn't *change* resolutions. So on my resolution paper, I crossed out the word *sweets* and wrote in *candy. I will not eat candy.* There. That was still a good resolution.

Soon it was my turn to go to bed. Mommy and Seth kissed me good night. They turned out the light. I lay in bed and thought. Sam had not kept his resolution. Kristy had not kept hers. Neither had Andrew nor Nancy nor Hannie.

I thought so much that I could not fall asleep. I kneeled on my bed and stared out the window. When I finally felt tired, I looked at my clock. The time was ten-fifteen. I was up way past my bedtime!

Uh-oh. *Now* what had I done?

Using a flashlight, I changed my third resolution to read: *I will not stay up past my bedtime, even to read. Unless I cannot fall asleep.*

CHAPTER 14

On January 11th, Mommy drove Andrew and me to the big house for the weekend. We had not been there since our long New Year's visit. I brought my notebook with me. It was getting pretty full. Andrew had barely remembered to floss his teeth. Hannie kept biting her nails. And I had *seen* Nancy write two notes and pass them to Hannie.

I wondered how the people in my big-house family were doing. I hoped they were doing better than Andrew and Hannie and Nancy. As soon as dinner was over, I decided to find out. I knew that Nannie was supposed to do some exercises and walk around with her walk Where did she exercise? I tiptoed aroun house until I found her in the family room. Elizabeth was with her.

"Just a little more, Mom," Elizabeth was saying. "Just a little more."

I heard Nannie gasping. "I don't think I can. That's enough for tonight."

"Okay. You did *really* well," Elizabeth replied.

I ducked into a closet. I opened my notebook. On Nannie's page, I wrote: *Jan. 11 — Nannie's not working her hardest.*

Then I snuck upstairs. I saw Charlie in his room. He was doing his homework. The phone rang then, and Charlie called, "I'll get it!"

I raced into my room before Charlie could see me. In my notebook I wrote: *Jan. 11 — Charlie talked on the phone while he was supposed to be doing his homework. He has been talking for four minutes.*

Boy. Couldn't *any*body keep their resolutions?

I hid my notebook under my pillow. Then I went into David Michael's room.

"Hey," I said.

"Hey," he answered. David Michael was

busy. He was drawing pictures of Teenage Mutant Ninja Turtles. "This one is Raphael," he told me.

"Nice," I said. "Listen, David Michael, did you practice your hitting and pitching today?"

"Nah," he replied.

"But that was your resolution. To practice every day."

"But it was *raining* today."

Back to my room. *Jan. 11 — David Michael did not practice today.*

I took my notebook and snuck downstairs. I heard a noise in the kitchen, so I flattened myself against the wall in the hallway. Then I slid toward the kitchen and peeped around the corner.

WHAT DO YOU THINK I SAW?

Daddy was taking a cake out of the refrigerator. He *cut* himself a *slice*. Then he sat down at the table by himself and ate the whole slice. Now how was Daddy going to lose ten pounds by April if he ate cake? Elizabeth was tryin help him lose weight. She was giving him fruit for dessert. But Daddy was sneaking sweets.

I raced upstairs. In huge letters on Daddy's page, I wrote: *JAN. 11 — DADDY ATE A PIECE OF CAKE AND HE IS SUPPOSED TO BE ON A DIET.*

That night I spied on Elizabeth. She finished everything she started. So *she* was keeping her ‎solution. But almost everyone else in the big ‎se had broken their New Year's resolutions.

Even Shannon, who had an accident by the front door, and Boo-Boo, who scratched Daddy.

Only Emily did not break a resolution. That was because she did not have one to break. And that was not fair.

I was disappointed in my big-house family.

CHAPTER 15

The next night I was very cross. On Saturday, this is what had happened:

1. David Michael did not practice.
2. Kristy talked on the phone with Bart about softball.
3. Elizabeth began to clean out the coat closet. She did not finish.
4. Daddy ate two cookies.
5. Sam burped.

I decided to do something about this at dinner. I took my notebook with me to the table. I ʻted until everyone had been served. Then ˥ up.

"I have an announcement to make," I said.

Daddy raised his eyebrows. "Yes?"

I moved to one end of the table and stood between Andrew and Kristy. I opened my book. "Nobody," I began, "has been keeping their resolutions."

"Their *New Year's* resolutions?" asked Sam. "I forgot about them."

"Well, I didn't," I said. "Listen to this."

I began to read from my book. When I got to

Andrew's page, I said that he had only flossed his teeth twice.

Andrew's face grew red. He started to cry.

"Andrew, why are you crying?" Kristy asked. She gave him a hug.

"Because," Andrew answered, "I made a promise, and I didn't keep it. And now everyone knows."

"Andy-Pandy," said Kristy, using Mommy's special nickname for him. "Don't worry. Nobody cares whether you kept your resolution."

"I do," I said. But Kristy did not pay attention.

"You just heard Karen," Kristy went on. "Practically no one kept their resolutions, Andrew."

Andrew sniffled and tried to stop crying.

"Anyway," I said, "Hannie has been biting her nails, and —"

"Karen, that's quite enough," said Daddy.

"Yeah," said David Michael. Then he sang, *Tattletale, tattletale. Karen is a tattletale.*" After that he added, *"Kindergarten baby, stick your head in gravy. Wash it off with applesauce and —"*

"Enough!" said Daddy loudly. "Both of you stop it. Karen, sit down."

Emily began to cry when she heard Daddy's loud voice. She thought he was angry. (Well, he was. But not with her.)

"Now see what you started?" Elizabeth said crossly to me.

I hung my head. Everyone ate quietly for a few minutes. Finally, I said, "And Emily didn't even have to make a resolution. We have to work — or try to work on special things — and she doesn't."

"Yes, she does," said Nannie. "She's learning English. And she's being toilet-trained. She's just too young to understand what resolutions are."

Then Daddy said to me, "Karen, look around this table. I see a lot of hurt faces. Andrew is hurt. And Nannie looks very hurt."

Nannie did look hurt. I felt especially b

about that. After all, she had been working. But she had said she would work *extra* hard. And I did not think she had done that.

After dinner, almost nobody would talk to me. Daddy and Elizabeth did say, "Good night," when I went upstairs to bed. And David Michael stuck his head in my room and called me a tattletale again.

Then Kristy came in and said, "Nobody likes a spy."

She did not offer to read to me that night.

At least I went to bed on time. *I* was keeping my resolutions.

But nobody else was.

CHAPTER 16

The next day, Mommy was going to pick up Andrew and me at the big house at four o'clock. At three-thirty, Daddy said to me, "Karen, I would like to talk to you before you leave."

This did not sound good.

"Where should we talk?" I asked.

"How about in your bedroom? Then we can be private."

"Okay," I said in a small voice. I was pretty sure I was in trouble.

Up in my room, Daddy shut the door. He sat in my armchair. I sat on my bed holding Moosie and Tickly very tightly.

"Karen," Daddy began, "I am not pleased with your notebook. You have been tattling a spying. Do you remember one of the rules in this house?"

"No spying on the neighbors," I said immediately. Daddy had made up that rule because I spied on Morbidda Destiny so much.

"Right," said Daddy.

"But I spied on our *family*," I pointed out.

"You also spied on Hannie. She is a neighbor. Besides, I don't like when you spy on anybody. Got that?"

"Yes," I answered.

"Good.

"Now, there are some other things I want to tell you. First of all, some people keep their New Year's resolutions and some don't. They try to, but maybe they can't. Or they forget."

"Okay. Can I go now?" I asked.

"No," said Daddy. "I want you to understand some other things. I know you like contests, but resolutions are not contests. There are no winners or losers. New Year's resolutions are mostly just for fun. People don't always take them very seriously. They are things to work on if they feel like it."

"Okay," I said again.

"*Now* you can go," Daddy told me.

"Thank you."

"Will you think about what I said?"

"Yes," I replied. But what I thought later, as I played in our playroom, was this: *I* had been very good at keeping my resolutions. I really had. I was proud of myself. And I had a long list of resolutions. I had kept them better than anyone else. Even if resolutions were not a contest.

At four o'clock on the dot, I heard a car honk outside.

Mommy!

I ran downstairs. To my surprise, Daddy was standing at our front door. He was calling for Mommy to come inside. So both Mommy and Seth came in.

Daddy said to Mommy, "I just want to speak to you in the kitchen for a few minutes."

I started to follow them, but Seth pulled r

back. "How was your weekend?" he asked me. "Did you have fun?"

"Yup," I replied. I was dying to know what Mommy and Daddy were talking about. But Seth would not let me go.

Darn.

Oh, well. I knew I would find out sooner or later.

Even if it meant spying.

CHAPTER 17

The next week was weird. Have you ever had the feeling that someone is watching you? I have. And I felt it plenty of times that week.

It is a very creepy feeling. It makes my hair feel funny.

Monday was when I got the feeling the first time. It was during reading. I felt like someone was staring at me from behind. So I turned around. But nobody was looking at me.

Then, on the playground, I got the feeling again. I was jumping rope by myself. When I felt eyes on me, I looked all around the playground. Everyone was talking or playing. Even Hannie and Nancy. They were nearby, but they

would not play with me. They were standing with their arms crossed.

"We're mad," Hannie had announced that morning.

"At me?" I asked.

"Yes, at you," said Nancy crossly.

"Why?"

"Because," Hannie began, "David Michael told me what you did last weekend. You told everyone at your house that I'm still biting my nails and Nancy is still passing notes. Now they all think we can't keep promises."

"Tattletale," added Nancy, just like David Michael had said.

And then Hannie and Nancy turned their backs. They did not speak to me much that day. In fact, they did not speak to me much that week.

At home on Tuesday afternoon I got an even creepier feeling than the feeling about being watched. I thought I was being *followed*. I was going up the stairs to my room. I whipped around.

I did not see anyone.

WEIRD.

There was one other thing I didn't like about the week. Ricky.

He had not asked me to marry him yet.

"When are you going to ask me?" I said on Wednesday.

"When I like you better," replied Ricky.

I could feel my cheeks burn. I was hur*

"What do you mean?"

"I mean, when you quit being the Boss of the World. You are not in charge of everyone, you know."

I guessed he was talking about my notebook.

I was beginning to wish I had never started writing in it.

CHAPTER 18

On Saturday afternoon, Andrew and I were playing in the little house. We were playing with our Christmas presents.

We had not worn them out yet.

Just as Andrew was smashing up another Dyno-car, Mommy came into the playroom. Seth was with her. Mommy was carrying a notebook.

"Karen? Andrew?" said Mommy. "Would you please sit on the couch for a little while? We want to talk to you."

I expected Andrew to cry. That is what he usually does when it sounds as if we are in trouble. Instead, he jumped onto the couch. I sat down next to him slowly. What was going on?

Seth sat in a chair, but Mommy did not sit

down. She opened up the notebook she was carrying.

"Karen," she said, "we want you to know that since last Sunday, these are the New Year's resolutions you've broken."

My mouth hung open. "What?"

Mommy answered me by saying, "You ate a lollipop after lunch on Tuesday. You did not always share your toys with Andrew."

"*Three times*," Andrew added.

"You only got a ninety-four on your spelling quiz," Mommy went on. "That means you made some mistakes."

"But I couldn't help it!" I cried. "They were hard words. And Ms. Colman did not tell us to study them. They were a surprise."

"You still broke your resolution, Karen," said Mommy. "And you broke a lot of other resolutions, too."

"How do you know?" I asked.

"A few little spies," replied Mommy. "Hannie, Nancy, Andrew . . ."

"Daddy always says no spying!" I exclaimed.

"I know. But I asked Andrew and your friends to spy on you this week so you could see how it feels. Do you like it?"

"No," I mumbled. "And I don't like being tattled on, either."

"I didn't think so," said Mommy.

"Were there any other tattlers?" I asked.

"Does it matter?" replied Mommy. "I just wanted you to know how it feels. I also want you to know that *I* know *you* *changed* your resolutions."

"*How?*" I demanded. "More spying?"

"No. I was cleaning up your room. I was collecting dirty clothes for the laundry. And under a shirt that was on the floor, I found your list of resolutions. You crossed things out. You added things. You *changed* your promises so that you could keep them. Do you think that was fair after what you did at Daddy's last Saturday?"

Oh, so *that's* what Mommy and Daddy had talked about in the kitchen.

"No," I whispered. "It wasn't fair. I was just trying to do my best. I made so many resolutions and I wanted to keep them all. I thought I was being good. But everything went wrong."

I felt terrible. I was embarrassed. I bet my face was red.

"Are you very, very mad, Mommy?" I asked.

"I'm mad about what you did. But I am not mad at you. You're my Karen, and I love you."

Mommy held out her arms. I got off of the couch. I ran to her. Mommy hugged me for a long time.

CHAPTER 19

After we finished hugging, Mommy said, "Karen, I think you need to apologize to some people. Don't you?"

"I think I need to apologize to a lot of people," I replied.

"But first I want to make an apology," said Mommy. "And I know Daddy apologizes for this, too. We're sorry we asked people to spy on you. And I'm sorry I read your list when I found it. We won't do those things again. We just needed to teach you a lesson, okay?"

"Okay," I replied. Then I turned to my brother. "Andrew," I said, "I'm sorry I embarrassed you. I'm sorry I spied on you. And I'm sorry I made you cry at dinner. I do wish yo would floss your teeth, though. It is a very good idea. It prevents gum disease. And —"

"Karen," said Seth, "I think you've said enough."

I nodded. And Andrew said, "That's all right, Karen."

"Mommy? I think I better call the big house," I told her. "Is that okay? I have a lot more apologizing to do over there."

"Go ahead," replied Mommy.

I went into Mommy and Seth's room. I wanted to close the door and use their phone. I needed privacy.

Ring, ring! went the phone at the big house.

"Hello?" said Daddy.

"Hi," I said. "It's me, Karen. Your daughter."

"Oh, *that* Karen," said Daddy, laughing.

"Don't laugh," I told him. "I called for a very important reason."

"Okay," said Daddy seriously.

"I want to apologize," I said. "I'm very, very,

very sorry I spied on you. And I'm sorry I read out of the notebook at dinner. I hope you have good luck with your diet. I bet you can lose ten pounds by April — if you really want to."

"Thank you," replied Daddy. "I accept your apology."

"Now let me speak to everyone else. Is everyone else there?"

"Yup."

"Okay. I'll take Sam first, because I yelled at him first."

Sam came to the phone in just a few moments. "Hi, spy," he said.

Just for that, this was my apology: "Hi, Sam. I called to say I'm sorry. I'm sorry you burp at the table and gross everybody out."

"Bye, spy," replied Sam. I think he was laughing.

My other apologies were nicer.

To Elizabeth, I said, "I'm sorry I spied and I'm sorry I embarrassed you."

To Nannie, I said, "I'm *really* sorry about what I did, Nannie. I know you'll be walking before the doctors think you will."

To Kristy and Charlie, I said, "I'm sorry I eavesdropped on you. I promise not to do that again."

To David Michael, I said, "I'm sorry I embarrassed you. But you know, you really should practice hitting and pitching more. Especially pitching. You are one of our best pitchers and the team needs you."

"Thanks!" said David Michael.

Then I asked to talk to Daddy again. "Daddy?" I said. "Will you apologize to Emily and Shannon and Boo-Boo for me?"

"All right," he agreed.

"And one more thing. I want you to know that I am throwing away all the mean pages in my notebook and I will never keep spy notes again."

"I love you, Karen," said Daddy.

CHAPTER 20

Boy, what a weekend. I have never had to say "I'm sorry" to so many people. I was very glad when Monday came.

On Monday, I walked into Ms. Colman's class. I was wearing my backpack and carrying . . . the notebook. The first people I saw were Hannie and Nancy. They were in the back of the room. And they saw me, too.

"Oh, *no!*" cried Nancy. "Look who's coming. It's the spy."

"With her notebook," added Hannie. She made a face.

I ignored what Hannie and Nancy were saying. I walked toward them. Hannie and Nancy ran into the coatroom.

I followed them.

"Here's the spy," said Hannie.

"I am not a spy anymore," I told her. "I still have my notebook, but I am not a spy. I'm through with that."

"What's in the notebook, then?" asked Nancy.

"I'll show you." I opened up the book. Each page still had someone's name at the top. And under each name I had written things. I turned to Nancy's page.

"Here you go. See for yourself."

Nancy took the book from me. She read, "'Nancy is one of my best friends. Nancy always shares. Nancy taught me about Hanukkah. Nancy got 100% on her reading test.'" Nancy looked at me. "Hey! These are *nice* things! Thanks, Karen."

"You're welcome," I replied. "Okay, Hannie. Here's your page."

Hannie read, "'Hannie is one of my best

friends. She is nice to animals. She always listens. She is working *very* hard on her cursive writing.'" Hannie thanked me, too. She looked really pleased.

"And I will keep adding things to the lists," I told my friends. "I will write down anything good you do. Or, like, if you win an award."

"Hey, what's going on in here?"

Hannie and Nancy and I turned around. There was Ricky.

"Oh, it's that notebook again," he said. He groaned.

I looked at Hannie and Nancy. Then I turned to the page I had made for Ricky. It said: *Ricky makes me laugh. Ricky does not tease me anymore. Ricky is the nicest boy I know.*

Ricky grinned. Then he said, "Gotta go. I just thought of something I have to do. Karen, don't come to your seat until Ms. Colman starts class. Stay in the back with Nancy and Hannie."

"Okay," I answered. What was Ricky up t

I found out on the playground. Hannie and Nancy and I were trying to make a snowman when Ricky came over to us.

"Karen?" he said. "Can I talk to you? Alone?"

"Sure." I left Hannie and Nancy. Ricky walked me to a private place on the playground. Then he held something toward me.

It was a paper flower. I guessed that was what he had been working on in the morning.

"Karen, will you marry me?" asked Ricky.

Finally! I thought. But all I said was, "Of course. Thank you so much, Ricky. Now we have to plan the wedding."

I ran back to Nancy and Hannie. I could not wait to tell them my good news.

About the Author

Ann M. Martin's The Baby-sitters Club has sold over 190 million copies and inspired a generation of young readers. Her novels include the Newbery Honor Book *A Corner of the Universe*, *A Dog's Life*, and the Main Street series. She lives in upstate New York.

Keep reading for a sneak peek at the next
Baby-sitters Little Sister book!

Karen's In Love

The day after I got the invitation to Pamela's party was another school day. Hannie and Nancy and Ricky Torres and I arrived at school early. We got to our classroom even before Ms. Colman. So did a bunch of other kids. But not ~~Pa~~mela. She had not come in yet.

"~~Y~~ou want to hear something weird?" Ricky ~~R~~icky has asked me to marry him. We will be planning a wedding soon. I think I love Ricky.)

"I always want to hear weird things," I told Ricky.

"Yeah," agreed Nancy, Hannie, Natalie Springer, and two boys.

"I got an invitation to Pamela Harding's birthday party," said Ricky.

"Me, too," said everyone else.

"What's she doing inviting *boys* to her party?" asked Bobby Gianelli. "I don't want to go to some girlie party."

"Well, what's she doing inviting *us*?" asked Natalie. (She meant herself and Hannie and Nancy and me.) "She doesn't like us."

"I wonder why we were all invited," I said aloud.

"Because my parents *made* me invite you," a voice replied.

I whirled around. There stood Pamela. Lesli and Jannie were with her. They are alw together, and they are almost always me

"My parents," Pamela went on, "said I had to invite everyone in my class. They said that was the only fair thing to do. Especially since I am new here."

Pamela joined our class after school began. Her family had just moved to Stoney-brook. At first, we were very interested in Pamela. She wears *cool* clothes. And her father is a dentist, and her mother writes books. Plus, she has a sister who is sixteen and lets Pamela wear her *perfume*. We all (well, all the girls) wanted Pamela to be our friend. But then we found out how snobby she is.

She proved it again right then. "*I* wish I could have had a sleepover just for my *special* friends," she said. She glanced at Leslie and Jannie. The three of them smiled.

"I wish you could have, too," I told her.

Pamela made a face at me. Then she and Leslie and Jannie went to a corner of the room ᴑ talk by themselves.

"Boo," I said to Ricky. "I know my mother ᴀke me go to the party."

"So will mine," said Ricky.

"Hey! Maybe we can jinx Pamela's party," I exclaimed. Then I lowered my voice. "You know, we can play tricks and stuff."

"Yeah!" whispered Ricky. "We can tell Pamela things. Like . . . like I found a spider in my piece of cake and now I am going to barf."

I laughed. "If we play Pin-the-Tail-on-the-Donkey, we should try to tape the tail on Pamela instead!"

"We can bring Pamela presents that look beautiful. But when she unwraps them, the boxes will be empty," said Hannie.

"Oh!" I said to Ricky. "Hannie and Nancy and I talked about presents yesterday. We decided to bring baby stuff, or things Pamela won't like."

"Good idea," said Ricky. "I will do that, too. What are you going to bring, Karen?"

"I haven't decided yet. It has to be just the wrong thing."

Ricky smiled. "Let's see. I could bring a snake."

"A *real* one?" I shuddered.

"Well, I was thinking of a rubber one. But a real snake would be even better. I wonder where I can get one."

Ricky and I could not stop laughing. We were imagining Pamela opening a box — and finding a snake inside!

Clap, clap, clap.

Ms. Colman was standing in front of her desk. She was ready to start class. She wanted to get our attention.

Everyone ran for their desks. We like Ms. Colman a lot. We try to please her. (At least, I do.)

Hannie and Nancy ran to the back of the room. They sit next to each other in the last row.

Ricky and I ran to the front of the room. We sit next to each other in the first row. That is 'ause we both wear glasses. (So does Natalie ger. She sits on the other side of Ricky.) I sit in the back with Hannie and Nancy.

Then Natalie raised *her* hand.

"Yes, Natalie?" said Ms. Colman.

"We'll give each other valentines, won't we?"

"Of course. We will each make our own mailbox."

That made me think of something. I would give Ricky a valentine surprise. But what? A gift? It would have to be something special. Extra-super-gigundo special. After all, Ricky and I were engaged.

So what could I get him for Valentine's Day? A bow tie? No, that would be boring. Candy? Maybe, but that was not very special.

Now I had to think of *two* presents to give to people. A yucky one for Pamela and a nice one for Ricky.

One Saturday I woke up at the little house. The first thing I did was groan. That was not because I had a stomachache.

It was because it was the day of Pamela

Harding's birthday party. Oh, well. At least I was not the only one who did not want to go.

I had finally found a present for Pamela. It was a package with five plastic bracelets in it: pink, blue, green, yellow, and purple. I knew that Pamela would not like them. I was not even sure they would fit her.

"Is this *really* what you want to take to Pamela's party?" Mommy asked me when we were in the store. "We could get something else. Or we could get something to go with the bracelets. Maybe a locket?"

"Nope. The bracelets are fine," I told Mommy. "They're perfect for Pamela." I took them home and wrapped them up. I wrapped them sloppily.

On the day of the party, I did not get dressed up. I just put on a pair of jeans and a baggy red sweater. I thought about wearing my party shoes. I wore my sneakers instead. Then I looked at my hair ribbons and barrettes. I did not put any on.

"Is that how you're going to Pamela's party?" Mommy asked when she saw me.

"Yup," I replied.

Mommy shrugged. "Okay."

Mommy drove Nancy and Hannie and me to Pamela's house. Nancy had not been allowed to give Pamela a Cracker Jacks prize. Her parents made her buy a game. Hannie had not been allowed to give Pamela the baby mittens. *Her* parents made her buy a pair of gigundo cool pants. They were pink leggings. And they were just Pamela's style.

Oh, well, I thought. Ricky is bringing a live snake.

Mommy dropped us off at Pamela's house and watched to make sure that we got inside okay. We had not been to Pamela's before. When we stepped into her house, it looked like a circus. Balloons and streamers were everywhere. A huge sign said HAPPY BIRTHDAY, PAMELA! A clown was walking around. And someone who was wearing all back clothes was carrying some paints. Everyone except Hannie and Nancy and I was dressed up.

"Hi," said Pamela. "Come on in. This is my circus birthday." Pamela looked very proud of herself.

I was so suprised that I forgot to say, "Happy birthday." So did Hannie and Nancy. We just handed Pamela her presents. Then we took off our coats.

I looked around for Ricky. He was not there yet. Boo.

I looked at the kids in the living room. All the boys were crowded to one side. All the girls were crowded to the other side. The clown was trying to make them talk to each other. He was not having much luck. I felt bad for him.

Soon the doorbell rang again. There were Bobby and . . . Ricky! Ricky's present looked like it was just the right size for a snake.

Since everyone had arrived, Pamela's sister came into the living room. "Let the party begin!" she cried.

What a party it was! The clown turned out to be a juggler. He juggled balls and canes and hats. He balanced a Ping-Pong ball on his nose. The person dressed in black came around and painted our faces. She painted me to look like a cat.

When the juggler and painter were finished, it was time to sit down at the special birthday table. The dining room was decorated to look like a circus wagon. There were goody bags at each place at the table, and boy, were they fancy. They were made of either red or blue cellophane, and they were tied with gold ribbon.

Pamela's mother and father brought in the birthday cake. We sang "Happy Birthday," and Pamela made a wish before she blew out the candles. I leaned over to look at the cake. It was the fanciest one I had ever seen.

Don't miss any of the books in the Baby-sitters Little Sister series by Ann M. Martin—available as ebooks

Want more baby-sitting?

And many more!

DON'T MISS THE BABY-SITTERS LITTLE SISTER GRAPHIC NOVELS!

AN IMPRINT OF

scholastic.com/graphix

BSLS